The Goffins
Puppets and Plays

The Goffins

Puppets and Plays

JEANNE WILLIS

illustrated by **Nick Maland**

WALKER
BOOKS

For Elise Neilson
J.W.

For Kathryn and John with love
N.M.

First published 2012 by Walker Books Ltd
87 Vauxhall Walk, London SE11 5HJ

2 4 6 8 10 9 7 5 3 1

Text © 2012 Jeanne Willis
Illustrations © 2012 Nick Maland

The right of Jeanne Willis and Nick Maland to be identified as
author and illustrator respectively of this work has been asserted by them
in accordance with the Copyright, Designs and Patents Act 1988

This book has been typeset in ITC Veljovic

Printed and bound in Great Britain by Clays Ltd, St Ives plc

British Library Cataloguing in Publication Data:
a catalogue record for this book is available from the British Library

ISBN 978-1-4063-2883-7

www.walker.co.uk

CONTENTS

THE CARRUTHERS

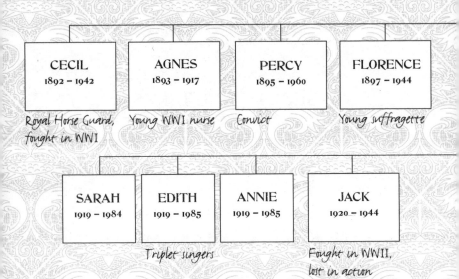

CECIL
1892 – 1942

Royal Horse Guard,
fought in WWI

AGNES
1893 – 1917

Young WWI nurse

PERCY
1895 – 1960

Convict

FLORENCE
1897 – 1944

Young suffragette

SARAH
1919 – 1984

EDITH
1919 – 1985

ANNIE
1919 – 1985

Triplet singers

JACK
1920 – 1944

Fought in WWII,
lost in action

FAMILY TREE

MONTAGUE CARRUTHERS
1870 – 1960
m
MAUD GOODWIN
1871 – 1971

Explorer, sailor, whaling ship

Suffragette, Titanic, WWI Nurse, maid servant called Violet, lived to be 100

SID
1899 – 1975
m
DOLLY GRAY
1900 – 1975

Joined army to fight WWI, under age, lost leg, won medals

VICTORIA
1901 – 1904

GORDON
1922 – 2005
m
PEGGY ELLIS
1926 –

Fought against Hitler in WWII as a young man

MARY
1926 – 2006

Evacuee

FRANK
1928 – 2003

Evacuee

SIMON
1958 –

PHILLIP
1960 –
m
SUSAN DERBYSHIRE
1966 –

Saved child from drowning

GEORGE
1999 –

Discovered Goffins living in his grandma's attic

THE STORY SO FAR...

George has a huge secret: there are Goffins living in his grandma's attic! Lofty and Eave belong to a race of people whose tiny island sank beneath the sea centuries ago. Homeless, their ancestors moved into the roofs of abandoned buildings, and now there are Goffins living in secret under every fifth roof in the country.

Like all Goffins, Lofty and Eave are skilled at recycling junk and have divided Grandma Peggy's attic into rooms furnished with bric-a-brac, stored there since Victorian times. Here, they survive on pigeon eggs, fruit from the roof garden, things Lofty fishes from Down Below, and any leftovers that George can sneak into the loft.

To his amazement, Eave knows more about George's family history than he does, from old letters and photos she has found. The more their friendship grows, the more George learns about Goffins, and the more he learns about himself…

CHAPTER ONE

GRANDPA AND GREASEPAINT

It was Saturday morning and George was in a foul mood. He'd hardly slept a wink, having been up half the night trying to learn his lines for the school play – they just wouldn't sink in. He had a dress rehearsal on Monday and the mere thought of it made him feel sick with nerves.

He was sure he was going to make a complete idiot of himself on stage and it had happened before. At his old junior school in London, he'd quite fancied himself as an actor and volunteered for the leading role in *Romeo and Juliet*. It was all going fine until

Puppets and Plays

Juliet went down
with chicken pox and
he'd had to pretend
to be in love with
a substitute Juliet
who liked to kick
his chair out
from under him
during maths.

As George stumbled through his speech, the substitute Juliet had hung over the balcony glaring at him and, instead of saying her lines, she'd scoffed and said, "Whatever. I am so not marrying you, loser." The audience fell about laughing and George, unable to speak or move, had to be dragged back into the wings by the teacher.

It had put him off acting for good, but here he was, cast in another school play. While the kids at his new school were kinder, he was still terrified that he'd miss his cue, faint, freeze or all three. With a shudder, he got out of bed and shoved his script into his school bag, only to find a letter from his drama teacher that he should have given to his mother weeks ago. Still in his pyjamas, George stomped down the three flights of stairs to the kitchen and waved it at her.

"Mum, it says here that you've got to make me a judge's costume by Monday."

She looked up from ironing Grandma Peggy's mountain of laundry and curled her lip. "*Monday?* You're joking. I'm working this afternoon and tomorrow morning."

"What about tonight? You never go out. You could do it then."

His mother shook her head. "Sorry George, I'm staying overnight at a hotel. It's a friend's fortieth birthday. I do have a life, you know."

"Can't you do it after the ironing?" pleaded George. "I need it for the school play."

"No," she said. "I've got to take Rex to the vet. He needs worming."

As if to prove her point, Rex climbed out of his dog basket and scooted across the floor on his furry bottom to scratch his itch. He looked so funny, George couldn't help grinning.

"I'll take Rex to the vet, Mum."

George's parents had only let him keep the little stray on the understanding that he'd look after him. He wasn't about to give them the satisfaction of saying he'd broken his promise.

"I'd better take him," said his mum. "You know how Rex hates the vet. It takes two adults to pin him down. If you want to make yourself useful, take this ironing back to Grandma Peggy

and see if she's got any cups to wash up."

George held out his arms to carry the folded clothes. When he'd first moved into Grandma Peggy's house with his mum and dad, he'd hated having to help out, but since meeting Lofty and Eave, he'd changed his attitude. Goffins thought nothing of doing a Kindness for free and George discovered that when he was nice to people, they were usually nice back.

He and Grandma Peggy hadn't been very nice to each other at first. But since George had made the effort to keep her company, he realized that she wasn't really an old grouch and she realized he wasn't a good-for-nothing pest. In fact, she often told him he reminded her of his Grandpa Gordon, her old husband, whom she'd adored.

Having struggled down the hall with the
pile of pressed clothes, a trail of elderly
underwear falling in his wake, George
elbowed open the door to Grandma Peggy's
bedroom. She was outside on the patio
scraping something from a plate into a basket
balanced on the bird table. George called
through the French doors.

"Hi, brought your ironing back!"

Grandma Peggy dropped the plate and
whipped round.

"Do you have to creep
up like that, boy?
I almost
jumped out
of my skin!"

Luckily, the plate hadn't broken. It still had remains of a fried breakfast stuck to it: a bit of bacon rind, a glob of egg yolk, some toast crumbs.

George picked up the plate and smiled. He'd suspected for some time that Grandma Peggy had been secretly putting out any food she could spare for the Goffins. In fact, he'd once been in her room when he saw Lofty lower his fishing line, hook up the loaded basket by its fancy handle and reel it back up to the roof.

He was dying for Grandma to confess, because then he could admit that *he* fed them too and it would be wonderful to be able to share the secret with someone. He could never do that though. He'd promised Lofty and Eave he wouldn't tell a soul they were living in the attic. They lived in dread of being caught. If that happened, they would have to leave and George would never forgive himself.

15

Even so, he couldn't resist trying to trick Grandma Peggy into telling him what he thought she knew, and now was the perfect opportunity.

"Grandma, who are you giving your fried egg to?"

"The G...oldfinches," said Grandma, going slightly red under her orange face powder.

"Doesn't it hurt the birds' feelings, feeding them egg?" teased George. "They're not cannibals, you know."

Grandma Peggy narrowed her eyes. "Yes, I *do* know. As long as it's not one of their eggs, the goldfinches aren't bothered. Now I'm going to ask you a question."

George's heart skipped a beat. Was she going to confront him about the Goffins and get him to be the first to admit they existed? She cornered him with her walking frame.

"W-what?" stuttered George.

"Why are you still in your pyjamas?" she said. "Are you sickening for something?"

George sighed with relief.

"Me, sickening? No, I've just had a terrible night's sleep. I've got a dress rehearsal on Monday. I'm a rubbish actor and I haven't even got a costume."

George went back inside to gather Grandma Peggy's collection of cups from under the bed.

"While you're down there, there's a red box. Fetch it out, would you?" she said.

George wriggled right under and hunted for it among the dusty paperbacks, hearing aid batteries and odd slippers. He also found a china pot with a handle, which looked far

too big to hold cocoa. George dragged it out and waved it at Grandma Peggy.

"I don't want the potty!" she hooted. "Just the box."

George couldn't wait to see what was inside it. He'd become very interested in his family's old possessions ever since Eave had shown him the hoard of trinkets and treasures in the loft, all of which belonged to relatives of his, going as far back as his great-great-grandparents, Montague and Maud.

George handed Grandma Peggy the box. She gave it a quick dust with her nightgown then flicked open the brass catch. The lid rose slowly on its rusty hinges.

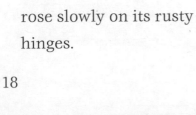

"You come from a very theatrical family, boy," she said. "Your Grandpa Gordon's sisters were a famous act."

She took out a handful of yellowing programmes featuring three identical ladies, smiling and kicking up their legs.

"They performed in music halls up and down the country – marvellous dancers they were. That's Sarah, that's Edith and that's Annie," said Grandma Peggy, pointing to each girl in turn. "Not that anyone could tell them apart, what with them being triplets. What did they call themselves, the Tip-Toeing Taps, was it? No, it'll come to me in a minute..."

George rooted through the rest of the box. Among the concert tickets, press reviews and pots of greasepaint, he found a false moustache and a tiny vial of theatrical gum. It was very crusty round the lid but when he tipped it, the liquid moved.

Grandma tapped her forehead and stared out of the window, still trying to remember the triplets' stage name.

"The Tap-Trapping Twits? No..."

George undid the vial, tipped it up and put a line of glue on the moustache.

"I've got it: the Toe-Tapping Trips!" announced Grandma. She turned to face George and burst out laughing. He had the moustache on upside down.

"You need a shave, boy! You're such a comedian, just like your Grandpa Gordon. Oh, he used to make me laugh..."

She trailed off, pulled a tissue out of her sleeve and dabbed her eyes. George wasn't sure if she was laughing or crying, and fiddled with the moustache awkwardly. He'd never known his

Grandpa Gordon. He'd died a few years back, but Grandma still missed him. Finally, she broke the silence.

"So, what are you in this play of yours, boy – a clown?"

"A judge," mumbled George. "Only Mum's too busy to make me a costume. You haven't got a black gown and a wig in your wardrobe have you?"

Grandma's eyes began to twinkle as if she was thinking up mischief.

"Have a look in the attic," she said. "There's a suitcase in there full of Grandpa Gordon's stage stuff: hats, cloaks, puppets... He was a Punch and Judy man after the war."

"I'm not allowed in the attic," said George pointedly. "Dad reckons *anything* could be in there..."

He watched Grandma Peggy's expression to see if she knew he was hinting at the Goffins, but she kept a straight face and played him at his game.

"I just heard your mum go out, and your dad will be having a lie-in, won't he?" she said. "What with it being Saturday. Then he'll be off to play golf."

George opened his eyes wide in what he hoped was an innocent way.

"Do you really think I should go in the attic when my parents have told me not to?"

Grandma Peggy cupped her ear. "Eh? Didn't hear a word of that, boy. Deaf as a post. Take the cups on your way out."

With his mother at the vet and his dad still asleep, George put Grandma Peggy's washing-up in the kitchen sink, grabbed the end of a loaf, a half-eaten jar of pickled onions and a small box of white chocolates. They

were his mum's – she didn't like white chocolate but George knew a girl who did, so he took them upstairs along with a fistful of toilet roll.

He went into his bedroom, pulled his day clothes over his pyjamas for speed and knocked on the green door that led to the loft, using the code he'd agreed with the Goffins.

Pom ... tiddy pom pom ... pom pom!

There were soft footsteps, the faint sliding of a bolt then Eave appeared wearing a Victorian wedding dress cut off at the knee. Usually she was delighted to see George but this time she took one look at him, gave a silent scream and slammed the door shut in his face.

CHAPTER TWO

JUDGE
AND JUDY

George crouched by the attic door, utterly bewildered. Why on earth had Eave been so terrified when she saw him? It was only when his nose started itching that he realized: he was still wearing the false moustache. He peeled it off and crouched down by the door, calling softly through a small split in the woodgrain.

"Eave? It's only me ... it's George!"

There was a long pause, then he heard her whispering to Lofty.

"Pappy? Himself be sayin' 'tis oh-nee Jowge. Darst us be openin' yonder door?"

"Nay!" muttered Lofty. "'Tis a trickster, pretendin' to be Jowge, us will be cotched! Trash and hide, Littley, trash and hide!"

From under the door, George caught a whiff of smoke as, in their panic, the Goffins blew out the candles in the chandelier that lit the attic. Now he could hear them shifting the furniture out of position. It was something they always did if they thought they were about to be caught, in the thin hope that the invader wouldn't notice the cosy rooms they'd lovingly made from a jumble of bric-a-brac.

George sighed. Right now, Eave would probably be hiding in the sailor's trunk that his great-great-grandpa Montague had brought back from one of his expeditions, and Lofty would be trying to make himself invisible behind the life-sized carving of an African king.

How could George convince them it was him? Maybe if he told them some stuff about themselves that no one else could possibly know? That might do the trick. George tapped on the door again.

Pom ... tiddy pom pom ... pom pom!

"Eave? Listen, I can prove I'm George. You're nine summers old, you have a brother called Arch who lives with your mum and Granny Cloister in a church belfry. You have a pigeon called Chimbley and a squirrel called Roofus."

27

There was no reply. Exasperated, George tried another ruse.

"I've brought you some chocolates..."

There was a little squeak of delight, then Eave opened the door, peered at his hairless upper lip, and flung her arms around him.

"Jowge, 'tis yourself!"

He opened his hand and showed her the moustache.

"Sorry about that," he said. "Forgot I was wearing it."

He showed Eave the groceries. Her gooseberry eyes grew rounder and rounder. She had a bit of dried yolk on her chin and George couldn't help wondering if it came from a pigeon's egg or Grandma's breakfast.

"Ooh, Jowge be fetchin' us choclick!" squealed Eave.

She took his hand and led him into the dark attic. Lofty re-lit the candles, illuminating hundreds of photos of George's ancestors that Eave had stuck to the walls.

"Got any pictures of Grandpa Gordon doing his Punch and Judy act?" asked George. "Grandma Peggy said there was a trunk full of his puppets somewhere..."

His eyes wandered to the far wall where Eave had stacked various suitcases, boxes and bags up to the rafters, all of which were neatly sorted and labelled in her own handwriting.

"Come sit, Jowge!" she said, straightening the faded lilac chaise longue in the room she called the parlour. "Be closin' your eyes. Myneself and Pappy be fetchin' a surprise."

29

Dutifully, George squeezed his eyes shut and waited. A few moments later, he heard the Goffins struggling back with something rather heavy.

"Nay peekin' Jowge," insisted Eave. "Us isn't ready yet."

It sounded as if they were trying to open a stubborn deckchair.

"Myneself shall be sayin' the laydee's parts, Pappy," whispered Eave.

"Right you are, Littley! Myneself shall be sayin' the man's and the crockydile's, yay?"

George was about to ask if he could look now when he heard the unmistakable words of Mr Punch, but in a Goffin accent.

"Halloo, boys and girls!"

George opened his eyes. There, in front of the mantelpiece was an old Punch and Judy theatre. He could see Lofty's backside sticking out through the curtain. Just then, the Judy puppet joined Punch on stage with a baby in her arms. Eave must have been standing on a chair to operate the puppet – she was really small for her age.

"Mr Punch!" she said. "Yourself must be mindin' the bubby!"

The baby flew across the stage, Mr Punch caught it.

"Nay, Judy. Myneself be too busy. Cotch the bubby!" laughed Mr Punch, throwing the infant high into the air and letting it fall to the floor.

"Alack, poor bubby! Myneself be callin' the policeman," wailed Judy.

The Goffins were putting on such a good show that George found himself joining in, especially when the crocodile tried to pinch the sausages.

"It's beh*iii*nd you!" said George.

"Oh nay, 'tis not!" insisted Mr Punch.

"Oh, yay, 'tis!" cried Judy. "Himself be munchin' us sausagins!"

There was a terrible murder, the police were called, then suddenly there was a pause in the action. George could hear Lofty and Eave muttering to each other.

"Pappy ... whyfor isn't yourself holdin' up the judge puppet?"

"Myneself oh-nee has two hands, Littley."

George went over to the stage and peered in at them.

"I'll give you a hand," he said. He crawled under the curtain at the back of the theatre and squeezed in between Lofty and Eave. When he put his hand inside the judge puppet, it struck him that his Grandpa Gordon's hand had been there too and he found it strangely comforting. He put the puppet on the stage and with a quick glance at the battered script stuck to the inside of the theatre, said his lines.

"That's the way to be doin' it!" said Lofty.

By the time the judge had tried Mr Punch for his crimes, thrown him in jail and taken a bow, George felt he was well on the way to conquering his stage fright.

"Yourself be a very fine actor, Jowge Carruthers!" Lofty said as he folded away the theatre.

"Am I? I guess it runs in the family," said George, who suddenly found himself looking forward to the dress rehearsal on Monday. Which reminded him – he still needed a costume!

"Eave, were any of my relatives judges? Only I need to find a wig and a black gown for the school play."

She tidied the puppets away and looked up. "Nay, Jowge. Not that myneself knows."

"Us has a judge in our family," added Lofty casually. "'Tis Grandmuppy Cloister, though herself be restin' now, what with bein' 103 winters old."

George noticed that Eave had a strange look in her eye, as if she was plotting something. He could almost hear the cogs whirring beneath her crazy mop of copper curls. She stood up excitedly and clapped her hands together.

"Yay! Grandmuppy Cloister be havin' a judge's costume yourself could have."

"Brilliant," said George. "But how could she send it here? Goffins don't use money so she can't buy stamps, and even if she could post it, it wouldn't arrive by Monday."

"Myneself be thinking' of another way—" started Eave.

"It's no good sending Chimbley," interrupted George. "I know she can carry letters but she's only a little pigeon. If she had to carry a parcel full of heavy clothes, she'd never get off the ground."

"Myneself wasn't thinkin' of sendin' Chimbley," said Eave, beaming at him. "Myneself was thinkin' of sendin' ... somebiddy else." She pointed to herself.

"You?" exclaimed George. "But you've never been further than Grandma Peggy's garden in all the time I've known you and even then you nearly got caught."

"Ah, but us will be travellin' under the cover of darkness, yay?" asked Eave.

George hated to disappoint her, but he knew roughly where Granny Cloister lived and it was too far to walk. "You'd never make it on foot," he said.

Eave refused to give up. "Yourself has a bicycool," she pouted. "Myneself can be sittin' on the hanglebars."

Lofty tipped the sailor's hat on his head. "Myneself shall be standin' on the pedils!"

George looked at Lofty in dismay. "Don't tell me you want to come too? I can't carry both of you on my bike. It's not possible to go by bus either, they stop running at midnight. We'd have to stay overnight at Granny Cloister's."

"Yay!" cheered Eave. "Myneself be goin' to pack a bag."

"No," said George. "This is madness. It will never work."

Eave's face fell. She threw herself back onto the chaise longue and pulled her frothy petticoat over her head to muffle her sobs. Lofty sat down next to her with his chin in his hands.

"Madness, Jowge?" he murmured, looking up with sad eyes. "'Tis madness for myne Eave not to be seein' her oh-nee muppy from one summer to the next."

Eave flipped down her petticoat. "And 'tis madness for myne pappy not to see his oh-nee wife, Ariel!"

She went back under her petticoat and carried on sobbing. Even Lofty looked as if he was about to burst into tears. George sighed.

"Listen, I know you both really miss your family and I'd love to meet them..."

They were gazing at George hopefully, hanging onto his every word. He was going to say that the idea of him escaping with them for a whole night was completely impossible, but he just couldn't bear to upset them.

"...so I shall think of a way!" he said.

Eave leapt up, Lofty threw his sailor's hat in the air and they were just doing a hilarious victory jig when George heard footsteps. They were coming from just outside the attic door in his bedroom. The Goffins froze.

George hadn't realized what the time was. His mum was back – he recognized her tutting.

CHAPTER THREE

BERETS AND BIKES

George held his breath for what seemed like an eternity. He could hear his mum gathering the vast collection of mugs he'd failed to bring downstairs and put in the dishwasher.

Finally, with a loud sigh, she left and he sneaked out of the attic and lay down on his bed. In a flash of inspiration, he thought of a brilliant way to explain the sudden sleepover.

"Mum, is that you?" he called, knowing very well that it was. She came back up the stairs and as he predicted, looked somewhat surprised to find him in his room considering she hadn't seen him there a few seconds ago.

"Where were you, George? I hope you weren't in the attic."

"The attic?" he said. "I'm not allowed, remember? I was under the bed looking for an invitation to that sleepover I told you about..."

"I don't remember," she said. "When is it?"

"Tonight," he said. "It's all right if I go, isn't it? You said I could last week."

George pretended to search high and low for the bogus invitation, muttering to himself. To his amusement, his mum got down on her hands and knees to help him look for it.

"Whose sleepover is it?" she asked. "Remind me."

"Hans Lofthausen's," said George airily. "My German friend from school. You remember him. It's his birthday."

George could see that his mother was struggling to remember Hans and this was probably because Hans Lofthausen didn't actually exist. George had invented him a while back to explain away a go-cart that Lofty had made and George had crashed. When his father had asked where the cart had come from, he had almost said Lofty, changed it to Lofthausen and added "Hans" for good measure.

"Everyone's going," said George. He had to persuade his mum to let him stay out overnight or the trip to Granny Cloister's would be doomed.

"OK," she said. "As long as his parents don't mind. I'll ring just to make sure."

"Don't do that!" blurted George. "The Lofthausens haven't got a phone. Well, they did have, but Hans's rabbit chewed through the wire."

"Oh?" she said. "Don't they have a mobile number?"

George struggled to think of a sensible reason why the Lofthausens didn't have a single handset between them but he could only think of a silly one.

"Mr Lofthausen won't allow mobiles in the house," he said. "He's a brain surgeon. He's convinced the radio waves interfere with people's thought patterns."

The lies were mounting up rapidly but his mother seemed to be falling for it.

"That's an interesting theory," she said. "Never mind, Dad can speak to Hans's dad when he gives you a lift."

"I don't need a lift," insisted George, jogging on the spot. "Hans only lives a few streets away and I'm trying to get fit. You always tell me I should walk more."

"I know, but you'll have your sleeping-bag and overnight things to carry," she said. "Dad will take you in the car. Ask him when he gets home from golf – he should be back in about an hour."

George wondered how on earth he'd conjure up a Mr Lofthausen out of thin air.

"I've got half an hour before I have to go back out," she said. "I thought I'd have a look in the loft and see if I could find something you could use as a judge's costume."

George leant against the green door in what he hoped was a casual way, in case she made a sudden dash for it and caught the Goffins red-handed.

"You don't want to go in the loft," he said breezily. "It'll be filthy – full of spiders. Anyway, my costume's sorted. Hans's mother is a judge. She's got an old wig and gown I could borrow. I don't know why I didn't think of it before...

43

Have you seen the time, Mum?" George showed her his watch. "Hadn't you better be going?"

George's mum still had plenty of time, but she seemed rather relieved to have an excuse not to scrabble round in the attic and she left, just as soon as George promised to brush his teeth properly when he went to Hans's sleepover.

George went downstairs to make absolutely sure that his mum had left the house and that his dad's golf clubs had gone, then he shot back upstairs and rapped on the green door.

Pom ... tiddy pom pom ... pom pom!

"It's all right," he called. "Mum's gone and Dad's out playing golf."

There was no need to worry about Grandma spoiling things – she always had a rest round about now and even if she was awake, her hearing wasn't good and she never came upstairs.

When Eave finally dared to open the door
to let George in, the chandelier candles had
been snuffed again. That was twice in one day
that the Goffins thought they'd been rumbled.

"Us darst not be too carefree, Jowge,"
mumbled Lofty. "Us does live in dread of
bein' cotched!"

He was about to relight the candles when
George stopped him. "There's no time for
that!" he said. "Not if you want to visit Granny
Cloister tonight. Are you both still up for
it? I've thought of a way but it
requires a lot of acting."

Through the smoky
darkness, Eave
staggered towards
him with a suitcase.
"Ourselves be
packed!" she
grinned.

George explained his grand plan about the fake sleepover. There was a cottage about a mile away that belonged to a teacher who'd gone on a school trip. Knowing it was empty, he would pretend it was Hans's house and ask for a lift there. His dad was expecting to speak to Hans's father but as he didn't exist, this was where Lofty would come in.

"Lofty, I need you to pretend to be Mr Lofthausen," said George. "In a minute, I'll take you to up to the cottage on my bike and leave you on the porch. I'll pedal home as fast as I can and by the time I get back here, I need you to be disguised as a French schoolboy, Eave."

Eave looked at him as if he was crazy. "But myneself be a laydee, Jowge!" She held out her petticoats and did a little curtsey.

"I know," he said. "But if I tell Dad you've come from France on a school exchange and you've been invited to Hans's, he'll give you a lift too."

Eave had never been in a car before – Goffins didn't own cars and they did not dare use public transport. Unless they had the materials to make a cart for themselves, they went everywhere by foot.

"Pappy! Myneself will be ridin' a *motor*!" she squealed, stuffing her fist into her mouth to control the volume.

Lofty didn't look too keen. "A Goffin be needin' a motor like a mermaid be needin' sandils," he grumbled.

"Don't worry, Dad's a very safe driver," George assured him. "Are you ready, Lofty? I need to get to the cottage and back before Dad comes home."

Although he was still jumpy from the morning's narrow escapes, Lofty put on a brave face. He swapped his sailor's cap for an antique felt yodeller's hat that Great-Great-Grandpa Montague had brought back from the Alps and, on shaky legs,

Lofty followed George down the three flights
of stairs to the front porch where the bike
was parked.

George pedalled off down the back roads
with Lofty standing on his stunt pegs. They
were wobbling like a couple of circus clowns
due to the extra weight on the back and it
was a miracle that they arrived at the
cottage
without
a crash.

"Here we are, Lofty!"
announced George, screeching to a halt.

Lofty had gone into shock. It was the first time he'd been on a bike and having rarely ventured beyond the loft in broad daylight, the combination of the two experiences completely overwhelmed him. George helped him off the bike, bundled him up the path to the cottage and sat him down on a stone bench near the front door.

49

"You stay here," George said. "When me and Eave arrive in the car and Dad asks if I can stop over, pretend you're Mr Lofthausen and just say 'ja!', OK?"

"Whyfor must myneself be sayin' 'ja OK'?" frowned Lofty.

"Just say 'ja', Lofty. It's German for 'yes'," explained George. "I'll be back as soon as I can, just don't talk to anyone."

As George raced home, he began to have serious doubts about his plan. So many things could go wrong, but now he'd set the whole thing in motion there was no turning back and he needed to apply his best acting skills.

He threw his bike back in the porch. There was no car in the garage, so his dad wasn't back yet. George still had time to help Eave into her schoolboy disguise.

He needn't have rushed. By the time he reached the attic, she was waiting for him in a pair of very long flannel shorts, a man-sized cricket blazer that she'd shortened with scissors, and a moth-eaten red beret, which she'd stuffed her plaits inside.

"Helloo, Jowgey!" she beamed. "Myneself be lookin' most like a scholar boy, yay?"

George tried hard not to burst out laughing. She was wearing the false moustache.

CHAPTER FOUR

HANS AND HANDSHAKES

When Eave looked at herself in George's bedroom mirror, even she had to admit that the moustache was a little over the top, but by then it had stuck fast.

"You're only meant to use a thin layer of glue!" exclaimed George as he tried to whip off the furry thing above her lip.

"Youch! Yourself be pullin' myne smile away!" complained Eave.

Rather than hurt her, George fetched a pair of nail scissors and trimmed the moustache right back so it looked as if she'd just got a bit of stubble.

"Dad will be home soon," he said. "If he asks, I'll pretend you came round to play on the PlayStation. If he talks to you, just nod or shake your head."

Eave looked disappointed. "Can't myneself even be sayin' halloo to Pappy Phillip?"

"No, if you do he'll realize you're not French," said George.

Eave harrumphed, then she sat down in front of his TV, grabbed the controls for his latest game and started pressing the buttons wildly. She'd only been in his room on rare occasions and was fascinated by all the modern gadgets that he took for granted.

"Whatfor be PlayStation, Jowge?" she asked. "Wherefor be the trains?"

He was just about to explain that there were no trains because it wasn't that sort of station when the front door banged.

"It's Dad! Come on, Eave," whispered George. "Remember, you are a French boy and whatever you do, don't speak."

George already had his pyjamas on under his clothes, so he just threw the script for the school play and a spare pair of pants and socks into a bag, slung his sleeping-bag over his shoulder then picked up Eave's bulging suitcase and led her downstairs.

"Myne legs be wobbilin', Jowge," she bleated.

Like all Goffins, she was perfectly at ease skipping across the rooftops but she wasn't good at climbing down stairs as she'd had such little practice.

"It'll be fine," George said whilst squeezing her hand tightly. "Fingers crossed, we'll be sitting down for a meal with your family tonight, Eave!"

George was really looking forward to meeting Eave's mother, Ariel, and Granny Cloister. He'd already met her brother, Arch, briefly one night when he came to borrow Grandma Peggy's mobility scooter for Granny Cloister to use. Arch had given him a Roman

medal for his trouble and it was one of
George's most prized possessions.

"Myne fambily will be normous happy to
be meetin' yourself, Jowge," bubbled Eave,
unable to contain her excitement. George put
his finger to his lips. He could see his father
in the hall.

"Hi Dad!" he said, over-brightly. "Good
round of golf? This is my friend, Yves."

His dad raised one eyebrow. "I can see
you're friends," he said.

With horror, George realized he was still
holding Eave's hand. He flung it away.

"It's alright, he's French,"
said George.

"Ah," said
his father.
"Bonjour,
Yves!"

Eave nodded so hard, George was worried her beret would fly off, exposing her girlish plaits, so he patted her on the head as an excuse to pin the hat down.

"He's a bit shy, aren't you Yves?" he said, glowering at her.

Eave – who was never backward in coming forward – glowered back at him and shook her head. George's father was staring at her bristly upper lip as if he were surprised to see such manly stubble on a schoolboy.

"He's *older* than me," blurted George. "He's only short because ... his dad's a jockey."

"Really?" said George's dad. He liked horse racing and often put a bet on for Grandma Peggy. "Where does your father race, Yves?"

Eave, who now wasn't sure whether to nod or shake her head, stared at her massive shoes.

"Dad! Yves doesn't like to talk about it," said George. "His father had a terrible fall so it's just as well we're going to Hans's sleepover tonight – that'll take his mind off it!"

"Myne poor pappy!" wailed Eave dramatically, pretending to dry her eyes on the sleeve of her cricket blazer and completely forgetting to keep quiet. George nipped her arm to remind her. Luckily, his father assumed she was speaking French and started to show off his own schoolboy French.

"Mais oui, pauvre Papa!"

Rex bounded into the hall to see what all the fuss was about and, seeing his little mistress out of the loft and apparently in despair, he threw his head back and started howling.

"Now look what you've done, Dad," said George, folding his arms. "You upset Yves and now you've upset Rex.

The sooner we go to Hans's, the better."

"How are you getting there?" asked his father, looking somewhat ashamed of himself.

"Mum said you'd give us a lift. I wouldn't normally ask but it's a bit of a walk and Yves's suitcase weighs a ton."

George felt guilty for making his dad feel rotten when he hadn't done anything wrong. They had never been very close until Lofty and Eave encouraged George to befriend his father, and they were getting along fine these days. But now he was accusing his dad of all sorts, so as not to undo the long line of fibs he'd strung together.

His dad fished the car keys out of his golfing trousers, picked up Eave's case and led them both outside to the garage. Eave could hardly breathe, she was so excited.

"Calm ... down!" George mouthed silently, stuffing his sleeping-bag into the car. He was about to climb into the back seat when his dad lifted Eave's case into the boot, the catch flew open and a frilly nightie fell out – the kind no self-respecting schoolboy would be seen dead in. His father looked at it quizzically then looked at Eave. George leapt to her defence.

"What's up, Dad? Never seen a French nightshirt before? All the boys are wearing them in Paris. Did I tell you Yves's dad is a fashion designer?"

George realized what he'd said and kicked himself. His father put the nightie back in the case and closed the boot.

"Thought you said he was a jockey," he remarked.

"He was, until he had the accident," insisted George. "Only Yves doesn't like to talk about that, remember?"

They set off and as George navigated the way to Hans's he prayed that Lofty hadn't got into trouble and was still where he'd left him. As the car turned the final corner and the cottage came into sight, George's eyes nearly popped out of his head. Lofty had found a pair of garden shears and was clipping the front hedge in the twilight. Even though he was standing on an upturned bucket, he could barely reach the top.

"Funny," said George's dad as they pulled up. "I'd imagined Hans's dad to be taller. He's not a jockey too by any chance, is he?"

"No," said George. "Hans said he played the flugelhorn."

"I'll go and introduce myself," said his dad.

"Why?" sulked George. "No one else's dad is checking up on them. Anyway, Mr Lofthausen only speaks German."

His father ignored him and got out of the car. "You know what your mum's like, George. She'll want to know there's a responsible adult in the house if you're staying over."

Out of the corner of his eye, George caught Eave giving Lofty a little wave. He hoped Lofty wouldn't wave back, not least because he didn't want his dad to notice and also because the bucket looked rather wobbly. He ran on ahead and tried to catch Lofty's eye.

"Hi, Mr Lofthausen. This is my dad," he said.

Lofty frowned and dropped the shears. For a few awful seconds, George thought he'd forgotten what to say, but then he slapped his thigh and said, "Ja!"

George's father held out his hand for Lofty to shake. Unbeknownst to George, the Goffin handshake was a particularly elaborate ritual that involved shaking the left *and* the right hand, then spinning right round and ending with a gentle slap on both cheeks. George's father wasn't quite sure what had hit him.

"It's a *German* handshake," grunted George. "You can go now, Dad. Please don't embarrass me in front of my friends."

His father put his hands safely behind his back and turned to Lofty. "I'll be off then – as long as you're happy for the boys to stay over, Mr Lofthausen?"

Lofty got down off the bucket, picked up the shears and snapped them together. "Ja!"

"Great. What time shall I pick them up?"

It wasn't the kind of question that could be answered with a "yes" in any language, and seeing that Lofty was about to say "ja!" again for the want of something better, George interrupted.

"It's all right, Dad. Hans's mum is giving us a lift back in the morning."

Glad to know that he could have a lie-in on Sunday instead of having to fetch his son and his strange little French friend, George's father finally drove off.

While George was enormously relieved that the first part of his plan appeared to have worked, he wasn't sure how Lofty and Eave would cope with the next stage. As he led them in the direction of the nearest bus stop, he hoped there'd be no other passengers waiting.

The Goffins had never been on a bus before.

CHAPTER FIVE

TICKETS
AND TAKEAWAYS

Luckily, no one else was at the bus stop, but
the bus was late. By now it was getting dark
and George's stomach had started to rumble.

"Would yourself be likin' a sammidge?"
asked Eave, rooting around in the front
pocket of her suitcase and pulling out
a parcel wrapped in an old bread bag.
"Myneself did make them."

"Is it fresh bread or birds' bread?" asked
George.

Lofty was often in the habit of sitting on
the roof and casting his fishing rod across
the lawn to hook up slices of stale loaf that

Grandma Peggy threw out for the wood pigeons.

"'Tis most fresh," said Eave. "Grandmuppy Peg oh-nee cast it out yesternights. Be yourself wantin' a honnee and prickled onion sammidge or a surprise?"

George didn't like the sound of the first filling, so he went for the surprise. It tasted absolutely disgusting but he forced himself to swallow each bite.

"'Tis most delicious, yay?" she smiled. "Is yourself guessin' the fillin'?"

It smelt like cowpats and tasted worse, but according to Eave it was fried pigeon's egg and white chocolate. George felt queasy. As the headlights on the double decker approached, he was worried he'd be sick on the bus. But this was no time to think of himself; he had to get the three of them on board.

The bus stopped. George pulled out a five pound note and waved it at the driver.

"Three tickets to Verulam Lane," he said.

George had a rough idea of the area where Granny Cloister lived from a map he'd seen in the attic and Verulam Lane seemed to be the nearest stop to the ruined church. After that, they'd have to walk off the beaten track and to the other side of a wood.

George had no idea how much the fare would be for himself and two Goffins and, to his disappointment, it was twice as much as he'd prepared for. The bus driver tapped the five pound note and put out his hand for more money.

"And the rest, son. One child and two adults to Verulam is a tenner."

"Ten pounds?" exclaimed George. "That's two weeks' pocket money! In any case, we're not two adults. Mr Lofthausen's a grown-up but I'm a child and so is she – I mean he." George pointed to Eave. "*He's* only nine."

"Nine?" grumbled the driver, staring at the remains of Eave's moustache. "Got an ID?"

"He's French," explained George.

"And I'm a Dutchman," said the driver, strumming his fingers. "Come on. I haven't got all day."

George searched his pockets for some change but all he found was a fluffy wine gum and an old cinema ticket. It was no good asking the Goffins for cash – they never used money. They swapped goods and services or did things for nothing, as a Kindness.

"Can't you take us as a Kindness?" asked George. "I'm not well. My French friend is taking me to see his mother. She's a doctor. If you don't believe me, ask Mr Lofthausen."

"Ja!" said Lofty.

It was all perfectly true. Eave's mum was a doctor and the egg and chocolate sandwich George had eaten was making him feel decidedly off-colour. He must have looked peaky because the driver gave in and, with a loud tut, let them on the bus and set off.

"Can us be goin' upstairs, Jowge?"

whispered Eave. "Myneself isn't likin' it Down Below." She'd just spotted some other passengers at the back of the bus and lost her nerve.

"Sure," said George. He stuffed his sleeping-bag and her suitcase in the luggage rack and was ushering Lofty and Eave towards the stairs to the upper deck when the bus lurched and sent them spinning helplessly down the aisle.

"Grab onto the poles!" cried George. Too late. Eave slammed into a mean-looking teenager, knocking his feet from under him. His takeaway flew up in the air, sending chips raining down on top of him as he lay on his back like a beetle.

Skidding on a greasy
chicken wing, George
ran over to help
them up, by which time
Lofty had been thrown
onto an old lady's lap
and was sitting there
like an overgrown baby.

Somebody must have
pressed the emergency bell
because suddenly the
bus squealed to a
stop. The driver got
out of his cabin and
marched over.

"He tried to nick
my takeaway!"
shouted the youth,
accusing Eave.

"Myneself never did!" she spluttered,
through a mouthful of chips.

"And driver, this man tried to pinch my

seat," insisted the old lady. "I think he's drunk!"

"Ja!" said Lofty.

George tried to explain what had happened to the driver.

"It was an accident. They just fell."

"Us isn't bus-savvy!" added Lofty, forgetting to be Mr Lofthausen. "Us doesn't have our bus legs, sir."

"Get up, you big lump. You're too heavy!" said the old lady.

Lofty got up gingerly and stood with Eave behind George. The driver scowled at them.

"Chips everywhere!" he said. "People sitting on each other! Any more pandemonium and you'll be off the bus, the lot of you!"

"Sorry," said George. "We'll go on the top deck out of everyone's way."

The driver yelled after them as they clattered up the stairs. "No ripping up the seats and no graffiti-ing!"

Thankfully, there were no other passengers on the top deck and the Goffins were far less nervous being up high. Eave sat at the front and pretended to drive, squealing with delight when an overgrown tree branch brushed the window. George leant back in his seat next to Lofty and tried to relax and let his sandwich go down.

"Thanklee for takin' us to myne fambily, Jowge," murmured Lofty. "Myneself be missin' them most terribil."

"I'm not surprised," said George. "You've been apart for ages. It's such a shame you can't all live together."

"'Tis sorrowfill," agreed Lofty. "But Granny Cloister be needin' Ariel and Arch and 'tis a squish in the belfry – there be no room to swirl a squill."

George was just wondering where he was going to sleep tonight if the church belfry was already too small to swing a squirrel, when he realized Eave was up to something.

"Eave, what are you doing?"

"Myneself be playin' a grand tune on this bus pipe, Jowge!" She pressed the red button with her thumb, making it ding repeatedly. "Din' a lin ... din' a lin!" she whooped. "Be singin' along, Pappy ... din' a lin!"

"Don't do that!" wailed George. "That's the button you press to stop the bus." Just as he spoke, the bus wheezed to a halt.

"We'll have to get off now!" moaned George. "And we're not even at our stop."

Eave's face fell and her eyes filled with tears. "Whyfor be myne step-in brother shoutin' at myneself?"

George felt awful. It was hardly her fault that she didn't know how to behave on a bus. "Sorry, Eave. I'm not cross with you. I'm just worried we won't be able to find our way to the church now."

Lofty patted his shoulder.

"Us may not be bus-savvy, Jowge," he said. "But all Goffins be star-gazey. Myne greatly grandplods be usin' stars to guide themselves around the Isle of Inish Goff way afore it sank beneath the Eye-Rush Sea."

"What if there are no stars?" asked George. "When I lived in London, sometimes I couldn't see any."

Lofty smiled. "The drabbest star do sparkle brightlee to a Goffin's eye, Jowge."

As they got off the bus, it didn't take a Goffin's eye to see that the night sky was scattered with stars and, with Lofty pointing out the various constellations, they found Verulam Lane in no time at all and were soon heading off towards the woods.

George
didn't like
to admit it,
but he was
scared. Being
a London
boy, he wasn't
used to the
countryside at
night and every time

a twig snapped or a fox barked, he imagined it
was the bogeyman and broke out in a sweat.

"'Tis fun, yay?" said Eave chirpily. "Us be
explorin' the deepest darks like your great-
great-grandpappy!"

When George first met Eave, she'd shown
him an ancient almanac she'd found in a
sailor's trunk. It had belonged to his great-
great-grandpa Montague Carruthers and it
was his record of all the exotic places he'd
explored, some of which were extremely
dangerous.

On rainy afternoons, George often sat on the faded chaise longue with Eave and studied the sketches Great-Great-Grandpa Monty had drawn of strange sea monsters he'd seen from his whaling ship, and wild jungle beasts, some of which were now extinct.

"Yay, Montague Carruthers. Himself be lion-brave, Jowge!" said Lofty. "Once, himself be almost swollied by a crockydile."

"Nay, Pappy. 'Twas a walligator," said Eave.

To George's knowledge – and he hadn't even read to the end of the almanac yet – his great-great-grandpa had also been attacked by a polar bear, strangled by a python and chewed by piranhas, and still lived to tell the tale.

It made walking through these woods sound very tame. Having reassured himself that the worst thing that could possibly attack him was a stinging nettle, George felt much braver. He started to whistle, striding along as manfully as he could with his sleeping-bag and the heavy suitcase.

Suddenly, Lofty stopped.

"Lo!" he said, pointing up through the trees.

Through the darkness, George could see the silhouette of a crooked church steeple.

"'Tis Granny Cloister's," gasped Eave.

She let go of Lofty's hand and broke into an excited run.

CHAPTER SIX

BATS AND BELLS

There was little sign that the church had been the site of an archaeological dig last year. The dig had forced Eave's relatives to flee to her great-uncle Garret's windmill to avoid being caught. Now the diggers had gone, the ivy had crept back and so had the Goffins.

Battling his way through the brambles in the overgrown graveyard, George arrived at a low wooden door at the back of the church. He was all for banging the knocker to announce their arrival but Eave held him back.

"Hold fast, Jowge. Myne fambily do live in fear of bein' cotched. 'Tis not a Kindness to be stompin' in without a warnin'."

Lofty felt in his jacket pocket, pulled out his twigaloo and blew a few haunting notes. It was a difficult instrument to play. Lofty had tried to teach George and had given him his own twigaloo that he'd carved from a branch overhanging the skylight in Grandma Peggy's attic. George could manage a few notes but he was nowhere near as good as Lofty, who could also use it to mimick the calls of animals and birds of all description.

He was making an owl cry now – but not any old owl cry: it was a code made up of hoots, rather like the code George used when he knocked on the attic door at home.

*Hoo ... hoo-ey hoo hoo ...
hoo hoot!*

There was no reply.
George looked at his
watch. It was only ten
o'clock but maybe they'd
all gone to bed early.

"Patience, Jowge," said Lofty. "Darst say
Arch will be answerin' shortly."

He blew his twigaloo again. High above his
head, George heard the distant creak of an
ancient window being opened. He stepped
back to see if he could see Arch. He couldn't,
but he could hear him; he was playing his
own twigaloo.

Hoo ... hoo-ey hoo hoo ... hoo hoooooot!

Arch was clearly thrilled that they'd
turned up out of the blue. As he played the
last note, he made the twigaloo sound as if it
was whooping with joy and in a few moments
he'd unbolted the church door and flung it
wide open.

"Pappy!" he beamed. "Jowge! Myneself isn't believin' myne own eyes!"

Suddenly, Arch's expression changed. He lowered his voice and took Lofty to one side. "Whofor be himself with the moustache? Wherefor be myne oh-nee sister?"

Eave threw her beret in the air and her plaits fell free.

"Here myneself be, Arch!" she exclaimed. Arch opened his arms and she buried her head in his cassock and hugged him round the waist.

"Myne oh-nee brother! Myneself be missin' you sooo much!"

When she could
finally bear to
let him go, Arch
led them past the
mouldering pews
and the dilapidated
nave to another low
door, urging them to
mind the chunks of fallen

masonry, and questioning Lofty all the way.

"Whyfor be yourself here, Pappy? Whyfor
be yourselves fleein' Grandmuppy Peg's? Fi!
Yourselves be almost cotched, yay?"

"It's nothing like that, Arch," George
reassured him. "I just need to borrow a
judge's outfit from your granny."

Arch stopped by the low door and looked
at George in disbelief. "Yourself darst be
travellin' all this way with myne oh-nee sister
for a gown and wiggin?"

For a moment, George thought Arch
was going to thump him for being so

irresponsible and he really hoped Eave
wouldn't mention the disastrous bus journey.

"It wasn't just for that!" protested George.
"I was going to come on my own but Eave
was desperate to see you all. She begged me
to bring her."

"Myneself did beg also!" said Lofty.
"Myneself be missin' myne Ariel most
terribil. Anyhoo, Jowge be takin' normous
care of us. Himself is knowin' us cannot be
too carefree."

"Himself be gettin' us into nay trubbil
whatsoever," fibbed Eave.

Arch looked at George sideways, then he
stopped frowning. It wasn't the first time
they'd met but it was the first time he'd held
out his hand.

"Thanklee, Jowge," he said. "Myneself be
most gratefill."

Honoured to have gained his trust, George
put his palm against Arch's and firmed
his grip. He was prepared for the Goffin

handshake, having seen his father on the other end of one. He remembered to shake the right hand and the left and although he span round a little late, he managed to plant the required two slaps on Arch's cheeks.

"Come!" said Arch, steering them through the low door. "Muppy and Granny Cloister be a-waitin'!"

They followed him up a spiral staircase. It was so narrow, George felt as if he was climbing round the inside of a snail shell and he was having a hard job bumping Eave's heavy suitcase up the steps, many of which were crumbling. Eave could see he was struggling.

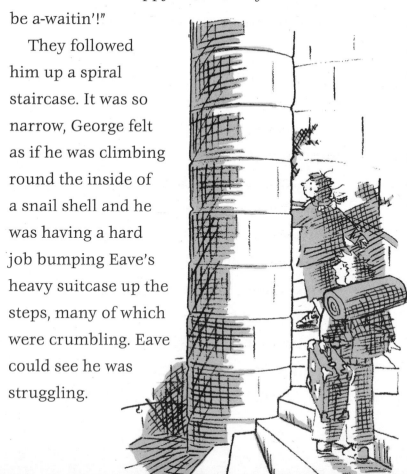

"Arch, please be carryin' myne trunk for Jowge," she asked. "Yourself be ox-strong."

"I can manage!" insisted George, not wishing to appear weedy in front of Eave's big brother. Lofty understood and backed him up.

"Is yourself forgettin' Jowge be a Carruthers, Littley? Himself be ape-strong!"

George wasn't sure he liked being compared to an ape, but it was clearly meant to be a compliment and gave him the extra boost he needed to drag the suitcase to the top step and onto the landing. There was a trapdoor above their heads. Using an agreed code, Arch reached up and knocked on it.

Pom pom-pom pom pom … pom pom-pom pom pom … pom pom!

George turned to Eave. "How come his knock has got more poms than mine?" he muttered.

"Now, Jowge," said Eave. "Arch be havin' extra poms but yourself be havin' more tiddles, yay? Fair be fair."

George knew he was stupid to be jealous but Eave worshipped Arch, and as much as he liked Arch himself, he wanted Eave to worship him as well. She wasn't his sister – he had no sisters – but she was the next best thing. George loved it when she looked up to him, and now he'd gone and made himself look petty and childish.

George needn't have worried. When the trapdoor opened, he soon redeemed himself by catching the rope ladder that Lofty missed as it fell through the hatch.

"Myneself be goin' first!" squealed Eave.

She sprinted up the ladder and, calling for her mother like a long-lost lamb, she disappeared headfirst into the belfry.

Lofty climbed in next, shortly followed by George. He was touched by the heartfelt cry of joy that Ariel let out upon seeing Eave. Arch stayed with him on the landing for a little while to give the reunited pair a few moments alone.

"Yourself be just in time for dinnin's, Jowge," he said, pushing his copper hair into a quiff. George was worried there wouldn't be enough to go round, given that Ariel had had no warning that there would be three extra mouths to feed. He wished he'd brought something.

"I didn't bring any food to share," he confessed. "We left in such a rush."

"Us be havin' plenty," Arch reassured him. "'Tis good fishin' Down Below. Myneself be haulin' a grand fungus crop a-growin' on ye olde tombstones."

"Fungus? Oh good," lied George.

Arch smiled goodheartedly. "Nay, myneself be oh-nee jestin', Jowgie! Us be havin' soup. Come, myne fambily be gaggin' to meet yourself."

Arch took the suitcase, balanced it on his head and climbed up the ladder. Having dumped it inside the belfry, he pulled George up by the hand, reeled the ladder in and, closing the trapdoor behind them, introduced George to Granny Cloister.

"Grandmuppy ... this be Jowge Carruthers!"

Sitting in front of him on a prayer cushion in a fourteenth-century bishop's chair was an old lady with a face like a walnut. She was barely bigger than a child and her white hair seemed to be permanently on end, reminding George of a startled Persian cat. She scanned him with her bright, gooseberry eyes and her face split into a smile as wide as a melon slice.

"Halloo, Jowge! Ourselves be meetin' at last. Yourself be most welcome!"

She seemed to be weighed down by the massive cassock she was wearing. It was decorated with lavish gold brocade and whenever she moved, she rustled. She held out her pale hand. Not knowing quite what was expected of him, George went to kiss her fingertips whereupon he found himself shaken vigorously by the right hand, then the left. As Granny Cloister span round and slapped him on the cheeks, he could hardly believe she was 103.

Just then, Ariel appeared with Eave in tow, carrying a gold chalice that had steam rising from it.

"Jowge! 'Tis most charmin' to be greetin' yourself!" she chirped, bobbing into a curtsey. "'Tis the besterly surprise myneself be havin' in long-along times."

She looked very like Eave only a little taller and a whole lot neater – she was wearing a purple dress made from altar cloth, trimmed at the neck and hem with several metres of choir boys' ruff. Ariel pulled out a chair for George.

"Yourself will be havin' some snail soup, yay? Myneself be breedin' 'em under a bible in myne roof garden. Themselves be most juicy."

Having only recently recovered from Eave's surprise sandwich, George wasn't sure if he could face snail soup, but he didn't like to be rude. He told himself that snails were a delicacy in France and sat down at the table. As it turned out, Ariel's soup was so much better than Eave's sandwich and he found himself agreeing to a second bowl as he drank in the surroundings.

To his left, there were a couple of wooden pews behind a wrought-iron screen where Granny Cloister and Ariel slept.

The kitchen was to the right. It had no door, just a few shelves and a worktop made from a lectern. From where George was sitting, he could see a stone church font, fancy as a wedding cake, full of washing-up.

The room was lit with church candles and moonlight. As George looked up, he noticed that there were niches in the belfry walls carved with the shadowy shapes of angels. Or were they devils?

He blinked. Was it a trick of the light or were they opening their wings and twitching? Then he realized that Granny Cloister had bats in her belfry – hundreds of them.

"Us be havin' a whole colony," said Arch, reading George's mind. "Themselves be fluttermeece, Jowge."

"I know!" he cried. "We found a baby one in Grandma Peggy's attic, didn't we Eave? It had hurt itself and we nursed it better."

"Yay, himself be called Gable," said Eave. "Does yourself be havin' any pets, Arch?"

"Myneself has a crow called Cloudier," he said proudly. "Herself be lovin' sparklin' stuff and be-fetches us many treasures."

He flashed the emerald ring he wore on his middle finger.

"Cloudier be findin' this and the medal our fambily be giftin' to yourself, Jowge."

"Arch be teachin' Cloudier to say halloo," said Ariel. "Like a parrit."

George was desperate to meet this marvellous talking bird, but of course it was night-time so she was roosting in her nest on the spire. He wished he could stay for a whole week so he could hang out with Arch and Cloudier, but beautiful as the belfry was, with its stained glass windows and statues of saints, it was certainly a tight squeeze.

Halfway through the soup, when he stood up to fill Lofty's goblet with communion wine, George banged his head on the huge bell that dangled over the table.

Instinctively, Ariel grabbed the clapper so it wouldn't clang.

"Darst say itself be gaggin' to chime," mused Lofty. "A silent bell be sadder than a tongue-tied lark, nay?"

Eave picked up her spoon and gave the bell a playful little tap. The sound was so sweet, George and three generations of Goffins were soon playing a rousing tune on it with the cutlery – loud enough to be heard inside the belfry, but not so loud as to alert Them Below, should anyone be trespassing.

This carried on for half an hour until
Granny Cloister thumped on the table with a
pepper pot and bellowed, "Or...der! Order in
the court! Whofor be wantin' to borrow myne
olde judge's wiggin?"

"'Tis Jowgey," laughed Eave, wiping soup
off the remains of her moustache. "Himself
be needin' it for a school play. Shall myneself
be-fetch it, Grandmuppy?"

"Thanklee, Eave, 'tis in a box by myne pew."
Granny Cloister peered at
George through the pair
of opera glasses slung
around her neck. "Be
yourself a famous actor,
Jowge Carruthers?"

"Himself will be,"
said Lofty. "Actin'
be runnin' in his
fambily!"

"I'm rubbish,"
sighed George.

The old lady raised her goblet of wine. "Let myneself be the judge of that," she said. "Be slippin' into myne gown and wiggin, Jowge. Us must be havin' a dressin' rehearsal right here, right now!"

Much as George wanted to get out of it, he knew he couldn't. Just like her granddaughter, there was absolutely no arguing with Granny Cloister.

CHAPTER SEVEN

SCRIPTS AND SCRAPBOOKS

It was hardly a full dress rehearsal given that George was the only actor, but afterwards he was very glad that Granny Cloister had suggested it. At first, he'd felt silly wearing her judge's wig, but it was amazing how dressing for the part improved his confidence.

He really got into the role and, with Granny Cloister's tips on character development and Ariel's demonstration of breathing techniques to overcome any last-minute jitters, George got to the end of his lines and was met with rapturous applause.

By then it was past midnight and, feeling tired but happy, he was glad to be shown to Arch's bedroom. Dragging his sleeping-bag, he followed Arch into the kitchen and through a doorway hidden behind a tapestry that looked as if it doubled-up as a giant tea towel.

Behind it was another flight of steps leading down to a small, semi-circular room in the tower. Eave held up her candle so George could get a better look.

There was a leaded window with a stone sill, and on the flint wall next to it there hung a portrait drawn in coloured inks of a man with wild hair and a little girl. Eave recognized them immediately.

"'Tis myneself and Pappy! Did yourself be paintin' it, Arch?"

He nodded. George was impressed; it really was a work of art. It had to be, because the Goffins had no cameras and therefore no photos of their family at all. George made a mental note to take a picture of Lofty and Eave on Grandma Peggy's old Polaroid camera when they got home. Chimbley could deliver it to Arch so he could see what their home was like.

"Yourself be snoozin' here," said Arch, taking George's sleeping-bag and laying it on the wooden pew that served as his bed.

"Are you sure? Where will you sleep, Arch?"

"Nowhere. Myneself be roof-fishin' tonight," he said, opening the window.

He took a home-made rod from under the pew, hitched up his cassock and climbed onto the roof.

"Comin', Jowge? 'Tis a full moon and goodly fishin' to be had."

George gulped. Although he managed to climb out of the attic skylight at home to join Eave, he still hadn't got his roof legs and always clung on for dear life. The church roof was much higher than Grandma Peggy's house – there was no way he was going out there.

"Another time, Arch?" he said, yawning dramatically. "I'm shattered."

Arch shrugged cheerfully and walked across the roof as if he was going for a Sunday stroll. George sat on the windowsill and watched as he cast his line across the churchyard.

"Whatfor be yourself thinkin', Jowge?" asked Eave, kneeling next to him.

"Your family are great," he said. "I can see why you miss them so much."

Eave rested her chin in her hands and sighed. "Yay, but as yourself be seein', 'tis too smincey for me and Pappy to be livin' here."

George looked at her fondly. It seemed unfair that so many Goffin families had to live apart simply because there wasn't enough roof space – even Grandma Peggy's loft was too small.

"One day, I'm going to buy a mansion and you can all come and live in my loft," he announced. Eave put her head on one side and smiled a small smile.

"Ah, yourself be dreamin', yay?"

"No, seriously," he said. "When I'm a famous actor, I promise that's what I'll do." He got his script out of his bag, kicked off his trainers and zipped himself into his sleeping-bag.

"Help me with my lines again, Eave. If I'm good on Monday, the dream might come true."

When George woke the next morning, he was still holding the script. Last night Eave had fallen asleep curled up at his feet while he rehearsed his lines, but now she had gone.

He got up and looked out of the window to see if Arch was still roof-fishing, but he wasn't there either. George rolled up his sleeping-bag and went to look for them.

All the Goffins were upstairs, sitting around the table eating breakfast.

"Goodly morn, Jowge!" said Lofty, patting the empty chair next to him. "'Twas besterly fishin' yesternights. Arch be hookin' a pricklepig."

"Alack, himself be squished, but waste not, be wantin' not, eh, Pappy?" said Arch, chinking his jewel-encrusted goblet against Lofty's, which for some reason had its top rim cut off.

"Pricklepigs be makin' a goodly breakfeast," said Granny Cloister, tucking in to her hedgehog rashers. "Us be savin' yourself some, Jowge. Ariel be frizzlin' plenty!"

Ariel handed George a metal plate. It was the kind the clergy used to collect money.

"Thanks, Ariel," said George, glancing at his watch. "But I haven't got time for breakfast. I'm afraid we have to go in a minute."

"*Go?*" said Eave, mournfully.

"I'm really sorry," said George. "But if we don't leave soon, Dad will be awake, Mum will be home and I'll never be able to sneak you back into the loft."

Eave pushed her plate away. She pulled her beret from her head and sobbed into it. "Uf-uf-uf – myneself be wantin' to stay with myne– uf-uf – *fambily*!"

There wasn't a dry eye in the room. George didn't know what to do or say. His own family wasn't one for weeping and wailing. He'd never seen his father cry and if he'd blubbed in front of his friends in London, he'd have been a laughing stock. But if you were a Goffin, it was different.

"W-hyfor isn't y-yourself a-sobbin', Jowge?" wept Eave. "'Tis oh-nee polite to s-sob when somethin' be so s-sad."

"Y-yay, 'tis good for yourself," howled Lofty.

Ariel held out her arms. "Come, yourself can be weepin' on myne shouldies, Jowge."

"'Tis the manly thing to be doin'," wailed Arch, mid-hug with Eave and Lofty.

It sounded like an order, so George let Ariel hold him and, to his surprise, he found himself sobbing – partly because it seemed rude not to, but mostly because he didn't want to leave any more than Eave and Lofty did. He was just getting into the swing of the Goffin sob-in when Granny Cloister banged on the bell with her fork.

"Order ... order. 'Tis now larfin' times!"

To George's amazement, the Goffins whipped out their hankies, dried their eyes and were suddenly all smiles, as if nothing had happened. Ariel sang as she cleared the table and George had to admit that he felt strangely cheerful after a good cry. Arch fetched Eave's suitcase and Granny Cloister walked them over to the trapdoor. Just before they left, Eave undid her suitcase and made an announcement.

"Muppy? Myneself be wantin' to give you this."

She reached in and pulled out a heavy book which she'd re-covered with fabric cut from an old silk curtain.

"'Tis myne almanac," she said, handing it to her mother proudly.

"Let me see!" said George.

As Ariel turned the first page, he saw that Eave had drawn his family tree and at the bottom she'd done a little portrait of him in watercolours and written his name underneath.

"Wow!" said George. "It looks just like me."

"Yay," said Eave, flicking through the other pages. "And here be sketchin's of myne houndbubby Rex, pitchies of Jowge's fambily … drawin's of myne boudoir … the view from us roof garden…"

It was a diary, a scrapbook, a wonderful record of her life with Lofty in Grandma Peggy's attic and their friendship with George.

"Us will be treasurin' this evertimes," said Ariel, clutching the book to her heart. "'Tis most precious! Thanklee, Eave."

She reached into her apron pocket, produced a velvet pouch cut from an old church collection bag and pressed it into Eave's hand.

"For myne Littley," she said. "From all ourselves. Arch be carvin' itself from the rim of a holy goblit yesternights."

It was a gold bangle encrusted with rubies. Eave's mouth fell open.

"Oh, 'tis most bootifil!" She thanked and kissed them all in turn, then slipped the bracelet over her thin little hand and showed it off to George.

"Look!" she said. "Myne fambily be givin' me a goldin wristlit!"

Lofty lowered the ladder through the trapdoor and gave Ariel one last hug.

"Come now, myne Eave. Us must be sayin' farewell."

They climbed down and waved until the trapdoor closed, then followed Arch down the spiral staircase and across the nave. Arch peered cautiously through a spyhole in the back door to make sure no one was around, then let them out.

"Safe travellin', Jowge," he said. "Be takin' great care of myne oh-nee sister, yay?"

"Always," said George.

He picked up Eave's suitcase – much lighter now she'd taken the scrapbook out – and with one last, bittersweet wave, the three of them hurried back through the churchyard.

The woods were no longer scary in the early morning light and the sight of rabbits and birds seemed to lift the Goffins' spirits no end. They made it to the other side of the trees in record time but when they arrived at the bus stop in Verulam Lane, to George's dismay the timetable said there were no buses for another hour.

"If we wait for that one, we'll probably meet mum coming back from her party!" he groaned. "And we'll never get back in time if we have to wal—"

Suddenly, he spotted a milk float coming down the road. It was the same one that did the rounds near Grandma Peggy's; he recognized the driver. If he could persuade the milkman to let them have a ride on the back, they might just get back in time.

"Lofty, we need to do some more acting," he whispered. "You're my grandpa, okay?"

Lofty took off his yodeller's hat and scratched his head.

"Nay, Jowge. Grandpappy Gordon be your grandpappy."

"Just pretend," said George. "You're my grandpa and you've hurt your foot."

Lofty rocked backwards and forward in his shoes. "Nay, myneself be standing on myne own two feet just fine."

Luckily, Eave understood what George was trying to do and as there was no time to explain to Lofty, she stamped on his toe. "Sorree, Pappy!"

Lofty yelled, clutched his foot and began to hop up and down like a demented wallaby.

"That's great. Keep limping just like that, Lofty..." said George, running toward the milk float.

After he'd had a word with the milkman, the
float parked up and George and Eave helped
Lofty onto the back. Then they sat with him
between the crates of semi-skimmed.

It was stop-start, stop-start all the way back
to Grandma Peggy's house as the milkman
went on his round, but it was a peaceful ride
and being early morning there was no one
about apart from the odd jogger.

"We're here. Off you get, you two," said
George. They grabbed their stuff and jumped
off the float onto the pavement outside

Grandma Peggy's. George watched for a moment as the float pootled off down the lane and round the corner.

"I can't believe it," George grinned. "We actually made it to Granny Cloister's and back without getting caught."

But he'd spoken too soon. He'd forgotten his door key. They were locked out.

CHAPTER EIGHT

BRACELETS AND BREAK-INS

There was only one thing for it; they would have to break in. There were no windows open at the front of the house, but Grandma Peggy always left her top window open at night. It was too small for George to squeeze through, but Eave might be able to.

George crept round the back of the house with the Goffins, furious with himself for forgetting his front door key. If Grandma Peggy was awake they were done for. He pressed his nose to the French windows and squinted through her half-closed curtains. She was fast asleep by the sound of it.

"Grandmuppy Peg be snortin' most heartilee!" giggled Eave.

"Shh! Climb onto my shoulders," whispered George. "When you get inside, open the door and let us in, OK?"

He crouched down so she could straddle his neck. Eave clung onto his ears as he stood up, then she let go, grabbed hold of the top windowsill and, putting one foot on George's head, she pushed herself up.

George was terrified that she would fall or get stuck, but Eave slipped through the window as smoothly as a seal through a hoop, and shimmied down the curtain. After a few seconds, he heard a faint click. She opened the French windows in Grandma Peggy's room and beckoned to a very reluctant Lofty.

"Hastilee, Pappy, afore herself be wakin'."

"Go on, Lofty," said George. "Quick, I'll see you in the attic."

Lofty tiptoed across the carpet, lifting his knees and wincing as if he was walking on hot coals. Eave and George followed behind. Lofty had just managed to escaped out of the room when suddenly the snoring stopped.

Grandma stirred. She sat up, stared at George and Eave and fumbled for her glasses.

"Is that you, boy?"

Eave bobbed down and scrambled under the bed. Grandma Peggy cleaned her glasses and peered at George.

"Ha! What are you doing in here at this time of the morning?" she said. "Been out on the razzle and lost your key, have you?"

George put Eave's suitcase down. Out of the corner of his eye, he could see Eave's foot sticking out, so he gave it a little kick.

"On the razzle? I wish," he said, rolling his eyes and feigning boredom. "I've just got back from Hans's sleepover." He lifted up Eave's suitcase as evidence.

"Oh yes?" said Grandma. "So who's your other little friend?"

Using the breathing techniques Ariel had taught him to help read lines from his script, George managed to calm his voice.

"What other little friend?"

"You know. The funny-looking lad in the beret and baggy shorts. He was standing right there in the middle of my room when I woke up just now."

Drawing on his acting skills for a second time, George gave her a pitying smile and patted her hand.

"Dear *old* Grandma," he said. "Your mind must be playing tricks. There's no one here except us ... see?" He made a sweeping gesture with his hand.

"There's nothing wrong with my mind, boy!" snorted Grandma. "It's razor sharp."

George looked at her sideways as if he clearly didn't believe her.

"You must have been dreaming," he said. "Sorry I woke you up so early. Why don't you go back to sleep? I could recite the lines from my school play ... that'll send you off."

Before Grandma Peggy could answer, George whipped out the wedge of paper and sat down on the edge of her bed.

"Act One, Scene One. Courtroom," he read. "Enter Judge, stage left."

By the time he reached Act Two, Grandma Peggy had slid down the pillow and nodded off. As her snoring reverberated around the room, Eave crawled out from under the bed. George rushed her safely up the stairs, then collapsed with relief in the kitchen.

Rex started barking and seconds later his mum came in looking dishevelled.

"Good party?" asked George.

She seemed surprised to see him home.

"Great, thanks. Pity I have to work today." She looked at the kitchen clock. "You're back early, George. How was the sleepover?"

He filled the kettle and lobbed three tea bags into mugs.

"It was OK," he said. "Bit boring, really. Yves enjoyed it though." He thought he'd better mention Yves in case his father said something. George was meant to ask before friends came round.

"Eve, who's she? I didn't know there were girls going." His mother raised one eyebrow. "I'm surprised Mrs Lofthausen approved – she was there, I take it?"

George pulled a face and tutted.

"Yes and anyway, it's not Eve, it's Yves," he stressed. "He's French. He's on a school exchange. The teacher put me in charge of making him feel welcome so I asked him round to play on the PlayStation while you went to work. Hope you don't mind."

His mother seemed rather pleased.

"Not at all. I think it's nice that you've got so many European friends," she said. "You'll be chatting away in French and German before we know it. Did Dad speak to Hans's father, by the way?"

George dropped his teaspoon.

"Course Dad did," he said. "Man, he's weird."

"Who, Dad?"

"No, Mr Lofthausen. He's really short, you know. His English is terrible but he's a good laugh. He does this really funny handshake. Dad'll tell you."

He finished making the tea and started hunting around in the fridge.

"What are you after?" asked his Mum. "Didn't you have any breakfast?"

George's mind wandered to Ariel's hedgehog rashers and he hid a smile.

"No. Mrs Lofthausen did offer but I wasn't hungry. She gave me a lift home though."

"That was nice of her. How's the rabbit?" asked his Mum.

"What rabbit?" replied George without thinking. He'd forgotten about that little embellishment and hid his head in a cupboard.

"Hans's rabbit," said his mum. "The one who bit through the telephone wires."

"Oh, *that* rabbit," he said. "I don't want to talk about it, Mum. It got electrocuted."

"That's so sad," she said. "Poor Hans."

"Poor rabbit," said George.

He'd got half a pat of butter, two croissants, a box of chocopops, half a fruitloaf, two cups of tea and a carton of orange juice, all of which he piled onto the tray with the fancy pattern.

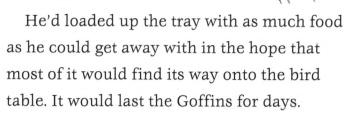

"This lot isn't for me," he said. "It's for Grandma."

He'd loaded up the tray with as much food as he could get away with in the hope that most of it would find its way onto the bird table. It would last the Goffins for days.

"George?" said his mum. "Did you manage to borrow a judge's outfit?"

She had caught him off-guard again.

"Yeah, Granny Cloist ... German cloth!" he said, trying to cover up what he'd almost said.

"The gown is made from German cloth."

"You'd better look after it then," said his mum. "I expect it cost a fortune."

She sat down and drank her tea while George carefully lifted the tray to take to Grandma Peggy. He could feel his mum watching him.

"Are you looking forward to being in the play?" she asked.

"I am now," said George. "I was feeling really nervous but I've learnt my lines and it really helped to meet a real judge."

"I'd love to see it," she said. "But I don't suppose you want your mum there."

She tried to laugh it off but she seemed a bit sad that he hadn't invited her. It wasn't that George didn't want her to come – it was just that he had always been scared he'd make a fool of himself on stage, so he'd never asked.

"Do you want to come, Mum? You can if you like."

She clapped her hands together, just like Eave did when she was excited.

"Ooh, yes! Do you mind if Dad comes too? He'd love to go. It'll be great, we haven't been out together as a family for ages, have we?"

It was true. When George was little, they used to go everywhere together – to the park, the swimming baths, the cinema. But as he grew older, things changed. When he lived in London, it wasn't cool to be seen out with your parents. He'd spent all his time hanging around with his mates, Warren, Dean and Jermaine, and when his mum and dad asked him to go to a museum or the theatre or the zoo, he'd roll his eyes and say, "Bor-ing".

After a while, his parents stopped asking. They went their way and George went his, but that wasn't the Goffin way. After spending such a brilliant night with Granny Cloister and the rest of Eave's family, George realized that maybe he was missing out with his own family, and wanted to make amends.

"You can both come!" said George. "It'll be fun to go as a family. I'll get Grandma a ticket too, shall I? It wouldn't be the same without you all there."

He smiled and went on his way with the loaded tray to Grandma Peggy's room. She was sitting by the French windows, listening to a play on the radio.

"Brought you lots of breakfast," he said. "Is it a good play?"

"Rubbish," she said, snapping it off.

George put the tray on her lap. There was so much food on it that she didn't seem to know where to start.

"The birds are going to enjoy this lot, boy," she chortled, glancing up at the roof.

"Grandma," said George. "Would you like to come and see me in my school play? It'll be much better than the one on your radio."

"Why's that?" she snorted. "Because you're in it? Your talking sent me to sleep earlier."

"Ah, but I was only *saying* the lines then, I wasn't acting. This will be the real thing: costumes, lights, music!"

"Will there be refreshments?" she asked.

"There's an interval with biscuits," said George, making it sound like the greatest treat ever. "Go on, Grandma. Mum and Dad are going. I want everyone in the house to come!"

Grandma reached into her cardigan pocket. She was hiding something in her hand. "*Every*one?" she said. She opened her fingers and held out Eave's bracelet.

"So ... that's ... where it went," said George, stalling for time as he tried to think of an excuse as to how the bracelet had got there.

Grandma Peggy held it up to the light.

"Found it on the carpet when I opened the curtains," she said. "How do you suppose it got there? Whose is it?"

"I've been looking for that. It's mine. Yves gave it to me," said George.

Grandma gave him a most peculiar look. "Eve? You've never mentioned anyone called Eve before. Is she a G...irlfriend?"

For a split second, George thought she was going to say Goffin.

"Girlfriend? Ugh!" he said, sticking his fingers down his throat. "No way, Grandma. Yves's a boy. He's French. He's here on a school exchange."

"Yves's a *boy*?" grunted Grandma Peggy, toying with the bracelet. "This looks like something a girl would wear."

George wondered how many more lies he'd have to tell to throw her off the scent.

"All the French boys are wearing ruby bangles this season," he said. "It's not really my style but it was a gift. I wouldn't want to hurt Yves's feelings."

He took the bracelet from Grandma and pushed it onto his wrist. Her eagle eyes spotted that it was far too tight for him and she wouldn't let the matter drop.

"You and this 'Yves' must be very close," she said.

"Closer than you'd ever imagine," mumbled George, gazing up at the ceiling.

Grandma smiled to herself and started buttering a croissant. If she knew George was talking about his favourite little Goffin, she didn't let on.

But then, brilliant actors did run in the family.

Goffin Dictionary

A

a-blowin' blow, as in wind

accibump accident

afrit scared

a-loney lonely

afore before

alack oh dear, alas

aloft above

amberlance ambulance

appil apple

B

be-accidents by accident

be-fall drop off, fall off

be-fallen fallen off

be-fetch retrieve, go and fetch

be-fix fix an item to something

be-guise disguise

be-morn in the morning

be-nights tonight, at night

be-scribe write

be-snuff snuff out

be-thunk thought

be-wilbered bewildered

be-yondertimes later on

besterly very best

betterly better than

bicycool bicycle

bide wait

binockles binoculars

biskies biscuits

bittilee bitterly

betwixt between

blam to hit hard

blankin's blankets

blisful lovely

bloomin's knickers/ underwear

boggyman bogeyman

bomb-fired blown up, as with a bomb
borned to be born
botticks bottom
bottils bottles
boudoir bedroom
bubby baby
bulltough strong
butteries batteries
buttyfly butterfly
brainhat helmet
breakfeast breakfast
broilin' boiling

C

candils candles
carefree relaxed
chamber room
charitee kindness
cheery cherry
chickeree chicory
chimbley chimney, also name of Eave's pet pigeon
chimbley egg pigeon's egg
choclick chocolate
choon tune or song
chrizzled christened
clamber climb

clangerin' making a noise
closet toilet
clucky egg hen's egg
cockerill cockerel
coddle cuddle
cometh is coming, has come
comftible comfortable
complicockled complicated
cotch, cotched catch, caught
cottin cotton
crafts skills
creepin' crawlin's insects, invertebrates
crewilly cruely
crockydile crocodile
crumpilled crumpled

D

dandyloon dandelion
darst not dare not
deaded killed

Goffin Dictionary

deadilly dangerous
demolishin' man demolition man
dentipeep dentist
dishin's dishes
dinnin's dinner
do-long year all year
dockyments documents
does do
doin's bodily waste
dread fear – also dreadfill
dressin' maker dressmaker
drownded drowned

E

ebidle edible
eekwill equal
endelong lengthways
evertimes forever

f

fambily family
fearfill scared
feathies feathers
fi! exclamation of fear, help!
fillum film

fluttermouse pipistrelle bat
foul horrid
foxsharp wily
frizzled fried
fruitibles fruit

G

gargled strangled
genteelman gentleman
ghoost ghost
gnits gnats
goblit fancy cup
Goff-cart go-cart
Goffin race of people from Inish Goff, now sunk in the Irish Sea
goggils glasses
goobies gooseberries
goodly great, marvellous
grandmuppy grandma
grandpappy grandfather

grandplods grandparents
greatfill grateful
grinnin' taking the mick
grisly horrible

H

halloo hello
hamsom handsome
hanglebars handlebars
hark listen
has have
hastilee quickly
hath it has
haul a fishing catch, as in a
haul of bird bread
head ouch headache
healthee healthy
heartilee heartily
hellishcopter hellicopter
himself he

hippopottimouth
hippopotamus
hither here, as in come hither
honnee honey
hook take, steal
horse sittle saddle
horse tack bridle etc
houndbubby puppy
hounds dogs
howfor? how can we
therefore?
hundrid one hundred

I

iggerant ignorant

J

jerkilee in a jerky manner
Jowge George
joyfill joyful

Goffin Dictionary

K

knickybockers bloomers

L

langwidge language
larfin' make fun of
larkswift swift as a lark
laydee woman
leaf sweat condensation, dew
lemmin'aid lemonade
lessins lessons
lionbrave fearless
littley child, kid
lo! behold
long-a-long very long
Lundiner born in London
lurgies disease

M

magifryin magnifying
marbils marbles
meatypaste meat paste
merrilee happily
merrimakin' having fun
mischeef trouble
miseree misery
moffs moths

morn morning
most very
motor car
munnee money
muppy mum
myne mine, belonging to me
myneself me, I

N

nakey without clothing
nay no
neighblies neighbours
neighbourly from the neighbourhood
newspapey newspaper
niddle needle
nightlie nightie
nightly at night time
normous enormous
nutriments nourishing food

O

oh-nee only, if only
olde old
olden-day diggers
archaeologist
once-a-time once
owlwise intelligent
ox-strong very strong
oziz ounces

P

pappy dad
parlour lounge
parrit parrot
peacefill peaceful
peacefun peaceful and
harmless
pedil pedal
peek to look, observe, study
peepil people
per-lum plum
piggy toe
pilloows pillows
plummet to fall
plumptious plump
plush soft
ponky smelly

'poon harpoon
pricklepig hedgehog
poppin' corns popcorn

Q

R

raidi-who radio
rare unusual, unlikely
rarin' urgent desire to do
something now
redded embarrassed
rellies relatives
riled angry
rillytruly to tell the truth
Roamin Roman
roly-round tied
roof-fish to fish from the
roof for food or items
roof legs to have no fear
of heights
rumpus noise

Goffin Dictionary

S

sammidge sandwich

sandils sandals

sausagins sausages

scarifyin' scare

screak squeak, scrape

scribblin's written matter, documents

serpent snake

shouldies shoulders

sicklee ill

skrike shriek

sky-dizzy afraid of heights

sky-like skylight

sky-savvy to know how to move around a roof safely

slew kill

slippins slippers

smincey little, small amount

sniff an odour

snitch nose

sockets socks

softlee quietly

somebiddy somebody, usually a woman

sorely painful

sorrowfill sorry

spewerpipe sewer

spookfill spooky

springly springy

squill squirrel

squish squash

step-in sister/brother substitute sister/brother

sunsit sunset

swede suede

sweetyheart girlfriend/boyfriend

swiftlee quickly

swollied swallowed

T

tastefill delicious

thanklee thank you

thus that is why, therefore

tiddlypoles tadpoles

'tis it is

to-gathered together

trash and hide to disarrange a place and remove traces of habitation

travellin' be-foots walking

trove treasured junk

trubbil trouble
'twas it was
twigaloo musical instrument

U

uncool uncle
us we
usefil useful

V

veggibles vegetables
vessels pots etc
villins baddies

W

walligator alligator
welly well very well
whiff to detect a smell
whumperin' whimpering
whyfor why
windyfone gramophone
wobblin' wobbling

woe misery
Worldly War One WWI
Worldly War Two WWII
wringle mangle
wristit bracelet
wype to wipe

X

Y

yalp yelp
yay yes
yearnin' hoping
yesternights last night
yestertimes yesterday or
in the past
yuletime winter
yonder over there
yourself you

Z

Don't miss the Goffins' other adventures!

Is there a Goffin in *your* attic?